AF163356

Agatha's Christmas tree

Claudia J. Schulze & Tim Holden

Table of contents

Agatha's Christmas tree page 4-49

The Christmas Concert page 50-58

Count Zeppelin page 59-65

Kazimir and the ring page 65-74

The Garden page 75-85

On the window page 86-88

The watchmaker's daughter page 89-95

Alyosha and Katya page 96-101

Hector page 102-105

©Claudia J. Schulze Offenburg-Strasbourg

Andrew Timothy Holden, London-Berlin

Michael Douglas Crawley (Lexington, U.S.A) und Vita Tucaite (Vilnius, Lithuania) ISBN: 9783743143593

Druck: Libri Plureos GmbH, Friedensallee 273, 22763 Hamburg
BoD · Books on Demand GmbH
Überseering 33
22297 Hamburg
bod@bod.de

Agatha's Christmas tree

The old woman, who everyone used to be a little afraid of at first, lived some distance from the edge of the town in a lonely house by the forest. Perhaps that was the reason people were afraid of her. On top of that, there was the fact that long after the end of November she still had carved hollowed-out pumpkins placed on her veranda.

In addition also Korax, an old, experienced raven, together with his splendid son, Krakan, and his strikingly good and beautiful daughter, Kiara, often would sit with her on the veranda. Kiara was particularly small but her eyes were much larger than those of other ravens. Krakan was, next to Kieran, the most splendid raven far and wide, and Korax was easily recognized by his once broken shiny, black wings. After all - a rather strange, lonely old woman surrounded by pumpkins and ravens that was enough to get people talking. Naturally they called her a witch, and not only privately, unfortunately. Of course they forbade everyone, and that included me, to ever approach her house.

Although I was almost 13 years old – and so almost grown-up – I obeyed that instruction to the letter. My fear was much stronger than my curiosity. At least up until the day when I first encountered Korax. In reality you couldn't really call it an encounter.

The raven never approached nearer than five metres. Whenever I took a step towards him he retreated backwards. I don't know why, but I kept trying again and again - and every time he moved back it looked like a strange, and yet not at all random dance, as if we had rehearsed it. Perhaps that is how it actually was

– at least as far as he was concerned – because in this way, as if he had planned it as a sort of game, he lured me with this dance as far as the house of the old woman. As soon as I saw the pumpkins on the veranda and began to understand where I was, I wanted to turn round. But Korax and the two other ravens, who were also sitting on the veranda, began to scold me in chorus, as if they could tell what I intended. Startled, I stood quite still. And there she was, coming out of the house. She didn't look at all like a witch.

Rather like a delicate, fragile doll with a skin which time had marked with thin, cute wrinkles all over her face. She gave me a friendly nod and sat down on her chair. Because she was small, her legs swung in the air. Nothing about her felt frightening. Quite the contrary. Just everything about her seemed to show a particular tenderness and kindness. I don't know why, but I sat next to her on the veranda. Next to the pumpkins there was still room for me and I am happy that I didn't run away that day. For how else would I have found out about the mystery of pumpkins and all the other things? The little old woman told me about it, and I had to promise her to pass it on to the world. She therefore told me about the mystery of the pumpkins and many other stories. Since she was very old, one day the chair in front of the house was empty.

Perhaps that has something to do with the fact that, to this day, I find it hard to look at empty chairs, because I still think back to that day with feelings of horror. Korax too died only a short time after her. Somebody had said that ravens could live to almost the age of sixty, if they only wanted to. I know that they can live to an old age but I have never believed the figure of sixty. But one thing was definitely exactly as I tell you. When Korax died, all the ravens from round about came to mourn his death. They sat in the trees around the house in which the old woman, by the name of Agatha had lived, and they croaked their sorrow loudly into the forest for all to hear.

Kieran, Kiara and I firmly promised each other to hold onto the memory of both of them and to share their stories with as many as possible. Each in his own way. It is not an everyday story and I feel that under no circumstances should it be forgotten and lost. Not this unique story and not this very special woman!

Even the time that I happened to steal her dented old blueberry-jug in the forest – she didn't hold that against me. I wanted to keep the memory of the old woman inside me.

Everything that she stood for. Of course it is a fact that deep down every person is something special. And so it follows that the story of every person should deserve to be recorded. But that falls outside the scope of what is possible for me. And so I am limiting myself to what I can actually do, namely to prevent this story from falling into oblivion.

Sometimes it is the only thing that someone can do. And if people sometimes feel that this isn't really very much I just must contradict them. I feel that it is something. Perhaps not a lot, that is true. But it is SOMETHING. And this SOMETHING can sometimes actually be pretty important. There was nothing that you couldn't talk to her about, and vice-versa there were also really no limits. Agatha talked about things that others would not have talked about so openly. In this way she talked about death. She said it was part of life and that there was no shame in mentioning it occasionally. But in this way she had not only made friends for herself. On the contrary. I personally liked Agatha so much, but many people thought that, especially in the presence of children, you shouldn't talk about death. Just as if it was something deeply indecent. Perhaps because people thought that children should be spared such things. And in a way that is hard to explain Agatha was always able to find connections between many things.

Perhaps that is to do with the fact that she simply understood everything. You could tell her things that you would have kept quiet about with other people. Like the time when I tripped over a stone and felt a little out of sorts. Who else but Agatha could you have told about it? So it was! She could put back together what would have stayed separated and broken.

Gradually the children in the neighbourhood came to love her. Although she was shunned by many other people, grown-ups in particular.

As happens everywhere in the world, the ban on visiting Agatha simply led to even more children approaching her house all the more curiously. But the parents knew nothing of this. Generally grown-ups do not appreciate people who differ too greatly from themselves.

Nevertheless. Exactly how she managed that I can't say to this day.

But the success she had in bringing the most diverse people together, this gift was still in evidence many years after her death.

Agatha, this was the name of the woman, listened to me mostly sitting contentedly on her rocking-chair wrapped in blankets, with her thin little legs dangling below her, as if she were a tiny old doll.

Her eyes were particularly clear and bright, and when you looked at her you knew that she was listening carefully to every word you trusted her with, and that she was one of the people who did not assume too quickly that they could understand you.

She took her time.

I could clearly tell that she was really taking the trouble to understand me.

And for this she took many long minutes and sometimes hours.

For that reason I also took trouble over her.

Not once did I try to seriously fob her off by saying something that was merely appropriate.

Not a single time.

Often hours passed in which we sat there together without either of us speaking.

You didn't have to pretend to be in a good mood or even amusing.

With her you could simply sit there. I liked that. Only the cawing of the ravens, who were often close to the house, sometimes broke the silence. This quietness and the peace there kept on attracting me to her and to her house. On some days that was particularly true.

One day during our weekly religion class such a strong feeling of anger had welled up inside me that I felt the need to call in on Agatha on my way home. Exceptionally she wasn't sitting in her favourite rocking-chair but was loudly banging nails in to the dark beams in front of her dangerously rotting veranda.

She was vainly trying to repair something. But when she saw me coming she stopped this, sat down next to me on one of the wooden steps and listened to me.

The religion class, in which the infinite power of God had been discussed, was weighing heavily on my heart. The words of the teacher seemed to me to be utter nonsense and I felt lied to by her. By her and by the whole world. Just not by Agatha. "*What a tiny light God is,*" I ranted. "*Great power, she must be kidding!*" "*He can't do anything! And when he can he doesn't want to.*" I had to think all of a sudden of all the misery, all the misery in the world and my own misery.

"*Well yes,*" said Agatha seriously
"*What most people don't know - and they don't like me for saying it – he is actually only a little light.*"

I looked at her in genuine amazement.

With adults this was not the sort of answer you would expect to receive. But Agatha would not let herself be fooled. On the contrary. As if to gather strength she continued banging nails into the veranda. "*He is a really small light in a whirlpool of darkness and suffering. But he is the only light that was there from the beginning. The only one - even if it is a small light.*" She looked at me attentively. "*Hey, can you pass me over the box with the nails. I need a few more.* "Finally, as she skilfully knocked the remaining nails into the rotten wood, she summarized her wisdom for me.

"*So,*" she began, "*there is something else that people should know. That has to do with the light and with the person themselves.*"
A few nails had to bear the brunt of this until she spoke again.
To be honest, I admired the strength and the determination with which such a small, fragile person could get this done. Even I at the age of thirteen was noticeably bigger than she was.

"The nearer you get to the light, the brighter it becomes, and in the same way the power that lived in this light can grow as well – together with you!"

She looked at me calmly then continued:

"God's power depends with certainty on our own. Our light strengthens him (or her) - sometimes in a roundabout way." She took another short pause and then continued:

"There just are no easy explanations for this.

Our understanding is limited and rotten, just like this wood here. And no more nails left anywhere ..." Sighing loudly and shaking her head, she contemplated the floorboards.
I looked at her clearly questioningly, perhaps rather obtusely, and so Agatha summarized everything for me again. She could do that well, for one of her greatest strengths was her

patience, apart from the skill with which she could stabilize old floorboards with a few precisely placed nails, not to mention her ability to listen so carefully or her great talent in dealing with crows.

"I only know that our light strengthens him, and that in the same way the absence of our light weakens him. So his power depends on us and also on the way that we deal with suffering and death, or with other people, with animals, with the world in fact. "I nodded.

Somehow that made sense. It didn't sound as theoretical not as so totally incredible as what our religion teacher had tried to make us believe. Agatha looked at me, thinking, as she often did, before she continued to speak:

"But what he is, just this small light is again more powerful than is mostly accepted. " So I tried to visualize this. "*He is there, he is a light,* and we will always be there – all the brighter the closer you are to him. He is perhaps also an it or a she – I don't think that is what is important."

I nodded. I thought so too. Such things were indeed quite incidental. Here again, Agatha held the same opinion that I did. "*It is the light that is important and we can all make it a little bigger throughout live*s*.* " Again I gave a slight nod and at the same time thought about what she had said, which wasn't so easy because she sometimes spoke faster than I could think. "*It is the same with darkness,*" she went on, and grew a little louder as if she wanted to give her words even more strength. It never grew loud around Agatha, except of course when children were visiting or when she was in the process of repairing something. But this here was important to her so that she suddenly spoke louder than usual. Just as if she wanted to make sure that it couldn't be ignored. Perhaps it was also because it sounded this time like a little sermon.

But I didn't hold that against her. If you are so convinced of something, you are probably also allowed to sound like a preacher. "*Darkness is always there. From the beginning. No one created it. It is simply there. Our task is not to ask why it is there. Some time we just need to lighten it. That is all.*" She said that as if it were not especially difficult. I still couldn't imagine what she meant. How should that happen? With massive neon-tubes or other gigantic light sources, lamps perhaps or an army of lanterns? "*You know,*" Agatha now tried to make plain to me, "*in the life of every person there is a sort of starburst hour. Perhaps these are more like starburst moments. They don't have to last long. But really, even when they only flash briefly inside us, they are important. They are moments when the being of the individual person leads to everything becoming brighter than normal for a while."*

I couldn't help thinking of my mother, of the first time with her that I could remember.

How bright and how warm she just made everything. I told Agatha about it.

She nodded. "*Yes that is part of it. And also your memory is a further light, because it is like a bright treasure that lives inside you.*"

I fought back the tears that threatened to well up in me.

Of course, I would have been able to cry in front of Agatha but right now I didn't want that.

Far more I wanted to understand what she meant. What she had already said, indeed, gave me something to work on, and very clearly this encouraged Agatha to continue.

"*Sometimes a single person has many of starburst hours, sometimes a few. It really isn't so important how old someone has become or how young someone has remained. It is only these star-bust-hours, this light that counts.* 'I now found this a little clearer and, when

Agatha went on to say that every person by their life contributes to making the darkness seem less impenetrable, I knew what she meant. Each of the hours of glory helped us to strengthen ourselves but also to strengthen the principle of the light. This made far more sense to me than what the teacher had said in the religion class.

But that is how is was with Agatha. She always knew exactly how to explain something so that I would understand it.

"Every single starburst hour counts, "she added, *"It counts just. Of course, as every single human being counts and continues to count.* "

Agatha also knew far more. That was one of the reasons that I kept calling on her before - some time towards evening, when the ravens were no longer crowing as loudly as before - I finally went home. Perhaps she knew so much because she was so old. Perhaps also because she knew what suffering was? What I thought the most probable was my inkling that it could have something to do with the fact that Agatha had already once been dead. That was nine years previously, so some time previously.

But still. For a whole two minutes and 57 seconds she had been dead. She didn't like to talk about it. Just occasionally she mentioned it. Perhaps to explain why she said things the way she did. Indeed, since then Agatha was no longer afraid of death. Quite the contrary, she said. Since then she was curious as to how exactly things would continue afterwards. That it WOULD continue, that she was convinced of anyway. That didn't surprise me. Nevertheless, how many people could say of themselves that they had already been dead for two minutes and 57 seconds?

That is why I always listened to her especially attentively and tried to understand why the lights, and the light always had such an enormous significance for her.

Indeed the idea of the lights came up in every one of her stories but without her hardly ever repeating herself. Rather it seemed to me that it was a special gift that she had, an immense, fascinating kaleidoscope which always provided new lights and new sights.

She once assured me that it didn't matter what you did in your life as long as it were something that was able to make this light a little greater. She said that the content of everything that we do would in the end shrink away and therefore no longer be important. What was however extremely important, this she emphasised in particular, was the attitude with which something is done. I remember that the word didn't make much sense to me. Attitude, for me that was the way that her body, that was not big enough for her chair, left her legs dangling like a rag-doll.

So she explained it to me again. She told me what she understood by attitude.

"You must do it with your whole heart, you must be convinced of it, and you must believe that the little light, even the smallest and most flickering can lead to something."

Saying that she gave me such a grave look that was enough to make me realize that this must be something very important. If you knew Agatha you realized that she never put on a serious face for no reason. Indeed mostly she would be laughing with her eyes and her whole person. Everything about her seemed to laugh, to sparkle and to beam. Sometimes I didn't know exactly what she meant - and at the same time in a way I did. I understood what she wanted to tell me. In a way it had to do with my dead mother and the fact she had also looked for the light. The fact that she had not found it, where I personally would have liked her to, did not mean – Agatha was sure about this - that the theory was contradicted.

I call it in a matter-of-fact way a theory, but I know that for Agatha it must have been considerably more than this.

But I digress. She told me that somewhere there was a great plan.

A plan that you cannot understand as long as you are on this earth. But afterwards you would understand it. Then you would start to understand how things were connected and that everything, indeed, was connected to everything else. "*There are many ways home, really many,*" she said not only once. I could

almost imagine her, equipped with enough needles and thread, embroidering just these words on a piece of material, so as to have it framed and hung up in the best room of the house. But since for most of her life Agatha had spent her life outside or in the hallway, where the piano stood, I have never seen the best room of her house. I could remember this saying without having this.
No embroidery was necessary.

Although I would sometimes have liked to have something to actually remind me of Agatha in a material way. Something you could touch properly like a picture, a piece of embroidery or just anything that had once belonged to her and had been particularly important to her.

But then I always realized that I would never need anything like this to actually remember her and how she was. "*There are many ways home*," I would always remember this and also what she had added to this: "*Sometimes it isn't the easiest way - and often it isn't the one that we would have chosen for ourselves - yes, really it isn't*". Once more she sighed a little.

"*Old people sigh a lot*," I thought to myself. But with her it didn't really worry me because she laughed at least just as often. Agatha, who one might think could easily say this because she was so old herself, also said that in the end it didn't matter if someone had had a short or a long life.

"*Some people are simply there for a long time,*" she once said, again very thoughtfully only to conjure up a smile from her serious frown, as only Agatha was able. "*But what we can pass on, the light – you don't necessarily need a long life to do that, do you?* " I absolutely wanted to know that. If only for the sake of my mother.

She thought for a little moment, finally she continued:

"*Perhaps you just have more opportunities,* "she said in the end. "*But that doesn't mean that you always use them.*" After a short pause she added: "*Many people who only have a little time use it in a wonderful way.*"

She then sank into one of her reminiscences. I already knew that.

I personally knew that Agatha' daughter had died when very young, and I also knew that Agatha, although she was already such an old woman, played with the doll which had belonged to her dead daughter. Not just that.

There was also still an old toy-horse standing on the veranda. But Agatha obviously liked the doll more. She dressed it, and sometimes she talked to it and held it in her arms just as little girls play with their dolls. "*You know,*" she said then, "*it was from my daughter that I learned that. She wasn't there for long – but long enough to teach me thi*s. "I believed her, and yet it seemed to me strange that she played with the doll, which she called Annie, just as her little daughter had been called.

Once, it was her last winter, I helped Agatha to decorate a Christmas tree from the forest. It was the first she had had for many years, she told me. A forester had given it to her as a present. The tree wasn't very big and slightly bent. Rather like Agatha herself, I thought.

But of course I didn't say so. Perhaps she might even have laughed at the comparison, but I didn't want to aggrieve her.

Just as it suited her, she didn't place the Christmas tree in the house. It stood with the pumpkins in front of the house and she decorated it with real white candles. These had not yet been lit, when the ravens settled themselves in the vicinity, clearly excited by the number of glittering silver balls, because Kiara, the lovely Kiara with the big eyes, came close enough to get a full picture of herself in one of the balls. Afterwards, when the candles were now alight and all the different silver balls reflected their light, they looked at them cautiously from a distance, keeping the whole scene in view. Curious as they now were, they looked on at what was happening - and this was unusual for them - in silence.

They had a style that was certain. I must say that it was something quite special, this Christmas tree of Agatha's that stood outside on the veranda shining such a fairytale light onto everything and transforming the forest that into something you could only have ever seen with her, and through her. This small crooked tree stood now with all its lights and illuminated everything with such a warm light that flowed back to me from Agatha's eyes like something warm, bright and good, like something that gave me the feeling that in some mysterious way everything would turn out well. For the very reason that she wasn't like all the others, I was constantly asking her things. Usually I am not someone who pesters other people with questions, but with Agatha it was different. "*So what is actually the sense in the whole thing?* "I once asked her. ""*The entire sense,* "Agatha answered, "*we can't always see that, when we are still here in this world.* "

She was convinced that it was necessary to fly some distance upwards in order to see life from a high vantage-point. Not until then, she promised me, would I understand everything. "*Even when you can't see the sense,*" she assured me. "*It is there.*" Perhaps, she suggested to me, perhaps it was just enough in life to just trust the fact that there was a sense – whether it could be seen, whether it could be recognized or not. "*Many things can be sensed, even when you can't see them.*" I stretched back my head and looked up.

"*Just trust in that,*" she said, with such conviction in her voice that it resonated inside me and created a sense of certainty that I previously never would have reckoned with. I thought of the forest with all its ravens and all those who could already fly in this world. On this day there was nothing I would rather have done than walk through the forest in order to see some of them.

And then, it was a brief thought, I would not have been surprised to see Agatha amongst those who, while still alive, possessed the ability to fly. On this day, I also considered, especially because of what happened with the doll Annie, that most people might well think that Agatha was crazy. But I myself didn't find her crazy. Not in any way. Not even during her last days, when she seemed a little confused and wanted to talk to me about the sense in life. Perhaps I shouldn't have kept asking her about it, especially not in the condition she was in. She was quite shaky and pale, almost translucent, which made her seem even more fragile than usual.

But something inside warned me that she would not be with me very much longer. It was such a feeling, a fear, a germinating sadness, something that was trying to warn me not to wait. I think this why I simply had to ask.

Who apart from Agatha could have given me an answer? However it seemed to me that words were suddenly useless to her. Not as if they had lost their meaning but had somehow changed.

"*The sense.... the sense .....*" Agatha reflected a little. "*I knew the sense once upon a time, when I was old or young or at the beginning of a new life ....mmmh*". She sighed "*But I have forgotten it*"

For a moment she had looked totally helpless.

"*I will remember it,* "she had promised. "*Some time when I am not expecting it.* "At this I had smiled at her almost encouragingly, perhaps this would help her to remember... And indeed: "*I think that once, yes, I remembered it again for just a moment*" "When was that? " I wanted to know. "*It was on one of those evenings that can sometimes be very dark, dark and lonely. I was sitting on the veranda and I no longer knew why I was doing that. Why I was sitting*

there at all. Then through the hollowed-out eyes of the pumpkin on the veranda, I saw those who were looking at me, but giving back or reflecting nothing. All was dark, but then there was this little light - even if that is all you can see. Just this little light. The light as a symbol of hope, a reflection of what is expecting us all one day. "She *sounds so funny today*,"

I had thought like this, which is not astonishing. "*Totally old-fashioned.* "Apart from that it did sound, to be honest, rather crazy and suddenly she was speaking without stopping but at the same time she seemed so weak. As if it were an effort to say anything. And then so many words, larded with long old-fashioned expressions that were not so easy to understand. And nevertheless I understood well what Agatha meant. Sometimes we didn't even need the same language for this. Agatha said something that still resonates inside me; perhaps especially because it was so soon before her death. She said quietly.

"Quite often I sit here on the veranda with the pumpkins and sometimes nothing makes sense any more. Then I don't know any more why I am here, why I was here," she sighed, "at all."
"Especially when I am alone and being alone feels worse than anything else. But then I see that in the end everything will be good." It was beautiful, the way she said that. *"You will see – it will be good in a way that in the end will seem to us quite obvious. It is the sense that we cannot yet see but that we can trust in."*

Now she became calmer again and actually looked more tired than before. I regretted a little having taxed her. But what she had said, I could now do something with. An inner voice had already told me something similar. It wasn't anything that could easily be put into words. Rather it was something like a feeling. A feeling that came from far away. From far away but also from a place that seemed to be familiar. As it were a long forgotten home. But something like that is better said to nobody. Nobody but Agatha. Here you could be sure that she also understood. "*Once,* "Agatha told me on one of her last days,

"*it was in the afternoon on a cold January day. I lay in bed and suddenly I was dreaming that I was a child and that this was the special midday nap before Christmas Eve.*"

She was silent for a longer moment and then continued, "*The midday nap before Christmas Eve was always the nicest of the whole year for me. My mother, my dear father, an older uncle, the grandparents, our dog Asco and the aunts all buzzed around the house. My three cousins were sleeping too, wrapped up warm.*

Everything smelled so good and in me I had this huge feeling of looking forward to the festival. It was the most beautiful moment of the whole year."

I still know that I just nodded. I could so easily imagine it all.

Agatha as a quite small, indeed a tiny girl (actually she never actually grew much bigger) the house, the lights and the people buzzing around preparing for the festival.

"Then," Agatha went on, "*I woke up. I was old, clammy and rickety. Around me there was no light, no warmth. It was a cold miserably dark January day. Christmas was long past and all the people I had dreamed about - every single one of them had gone. Dead long before me. When I awoke and realized this, it was terrible.*

In the beginning. 'She looked at me sadly as if she had just been roughly reminded of something. In the end she pulled herself together a little and went on:

"But all at once I realized that my death would be like this. Just like it. Like my midday nap before the Christmas festival. And I would see them all there afterwards. All of them." A look of joyful anticipation showed on Agatha's face.

Such a look of joy that I indeed had to think of Christmas. I remember exactly that I all at once I sat down closer to Agatha. Perhaps because I suddenly felt a slight fear of the inevitable day when she would no longer be with me.

But the joy on the face of this old woman, who had grown so important to me, was growing and it grew stronger than my fear, and in the end I only though of Christmas and to what, when my mother was still alive, I had always liked about it the most. Looking forward to it. In the days after Agatha's death, when I was sometimes very angry with her. Because she had left me alone, I could no longer thing about this looking forward. Her death had linked itself to the incomprehensible death of my mother and now I felt this weight with twice the dismal heaviness.

It was as if every feeling were extinguished, as bare as a Christmas tree that that someone had simply forgotten to decorate or at least to finally dispose of. Because the dismal Christmas tree of my imagination was already dropping its needles.

It was without any decorations and not even green any more. Just a brown, thin skeleton that was without life and without joy. It was like me. For a long time. I can't exactly say when that changed. Perhaps it took a winter, more likely two or three, because never again have I met a person like Agatha. I don't know whether I can believe that I will really see her again, her or my mother. I know Agatha would me mortified to learn that there was ever a single second when I could doubt this.

People like her - you, shouldn't upset them with such thoughts. That much I knew already. And that is probably the reason that since then I have decorated a Christmas tree every year. Mostly it stayed with us until Easter.

Just as Agatha never managed to clear away her November pumpkins, in the same way I found it hard to part with my Christmas trees. More than once my family has raised this with me, and one day my children didn't want to let anyone into the house because this Christmas tree at Easter was embarrassing for them. On this day I told them about Agatha for the first time, because I thought they were now old enough to understand why people sometimes find it hard to part with things. Especially something that is beautiful, that gives you light and a little joy. At first I didn't know if my children had understood that. But then they began to keep asking about Agatha, also about Kieran, Kraken, Korax and Kiara, the raven who had first led me to her, and I had to tell them about her. About her veranda on which the pumpkins were placed next to her chair, about the ravens in the forest who were so attached to each other and also mourned Agatha so copiously.

Seemingly, Agatha appeared to my children like a magical being, so much did they want to know about her. The more I told about her, the more she appeared to me as well as this fabulous magical figure, yet of course she wasn't. She was a person. In a special sense she had made life magical for me, and perhaps this is why my children elevated her to this status.

Finally they persuaded me to hang little paper ravens on our Christmas tree. From this year on, not one raven was ever missing from our tree. From this time on, my children only ever called it Agatha's Christmas tree, and it didn't worry them any more if it stood long after it's time in our living room because it was nothing less than *Agatha's* Christmas tree. With its lights and now also with the ravens it brought so much good to our home. Just as my dear Agatha, back then, had brought so much good to my life. I often reflect on the fact that I have a raven to thank for our acquaintance. A creature that in our parts does not enjoy a good reputation. Unfairly, in many respects. How wrong you can be, when you only listen to what other people say or when you stop looking or listening carefully for yourself?

That was something else I learned from meeting Agatha. She never expressed these things directly, but her whole way of being taught it to me. Whenever I talked about her I felt limitlessly rich from the gift of having known her. I can see her in front of me so clearly. I still don't know whether I can believe that I will be able to see her again. But she gave me something that now always stays with me. When she once told me that is far easier for darkness to spread, because this needed far less energy, that is was almost an automatic law of nature that darkness could spread far more deeply and far more quickly than it would be possible for light to do; that on the other hand only one single light was sufficient to make the darkness less dark and thus

prevent it from being total darkness. Then I must say that, for me, she was one of these lights. Even in the hardest and darkest hours of my life she was always with me. Whenever I thought - and still do think - of her certainty and of her joyful looking forward, then I feel born along by it. Born along by the certainty, which suddenly grew so firm in that year, that I would not wake up to a cold January day in the middle of nowhere, but shortly before the beginning of a solemnly Christmas celebration, surrounded by all those that I had ever loved.

The Christmas Concert

I remember one of the concerts that was given at Christmas. Outside there were terrible snowdrifts and I was not sure whether many people would actually come. "Concert by Candlelight" – so it had been advertised, and along with it there were to be tea and cakes.

Helpers had prepared everything and even put out blankets in the church, which also served as the concert hall. That would not have been necessary. This church was normally warm; a prudent architect had clearly thought about this at the very beginning. Myself, the clarinettist, and the young woman with the bassoon sat nervously near the altar. I was directly next to the concert grand piano which had been generously loaned by a wealthy music-lover and which certainly would not have been drowned by the sounds of the

Silbermann organ. But today the organ would remain silent. We alone, at the front of the church, were to provide a suitably festive atmosphere.

But would anyone actually come? Would the rehearsals of the last few days simply be art for art's sake without ever being performed for an audience? "*You have no idea how many people have absolutely nobody, especially at Christmas.*" The pastor assured us emphatically. "*They will turn up whatever the weather!*" Well you would expect a pastor to be so optimistic. But we found it increasingly difficult. We - still - just as unsure, drank our tea and tactically tried to hide our nervousness from the others.

The church bells rang out with a full, soft sound. Then there was a cold blast of air and the door opened and did not close again for quite some time. The pastor chuckled, rather pleased with himself for the prediction he had just made. People were streaming in such numbers that we never could have imagined.

We waited until the church clock had chimed the quarter-hour and then our concert began. Many people had arrived and they now sat, exhausted by the journey still stiff and uncomfortable in their seats.

The melting snow transformed itself into little puddles at their feet. Their faces, although I was trying to concentrate on playing, seemed stiff, as if they were frozen. But as we played something changed. This metamorphosis took some time, but I observed it in all its nuances and facets. After we had played for a good hour in the light of the candles, the stiffness in the faces of the people had given way to something quite different. Something like a glow now lay on their faces and made it clear to me - once more – why I had chosen this profession.

"*Peace be with you,*" murmured the pastor. But this peace required no words from him.
Often in the past I had thought that I was playing for just one person alone.

For the one person in the audience who really understood my music. I am aware of the fact that this could sound arrogant, but it isn't intended that way. Only sometimes, when I could no longer fight the impression that many people in the audience only came to a concert to be seen there, to present themselves as belonging to the educated middle-class or to get away from the loneliness of a rainy Sunday, it was at those times that this thought obtruded on me. But today it was different. Today I played, we played, for everyone here in the room. Meanwhile the storm grew ever louder, ever more difficult to ignore. With our instruments, with the candles and even with the Christmas tree that stood next to the pulpit we tried to distract people from it. We succeeded in this for quite some time but towards the end of the concert we had to resign ourselves to the fact that the sounds of nature, threatening and loud, were now intruding into our safe space.

With the best will in the world, I could not imagine how all these people were to get home safely. What would happen to the glow on their faces and the peace in their hearts?

Well that would have been the least of their worries. Even the pastor, who - in contrast to his normal manner - had kept himself very much in the background grew uneasy. It could have been a sort of stereotypical occupational disease, but the pastor really did worry about all the people who had come to listen to the Christmas concert in his church. After we had finished the last piece and the applause had ebbed away the pastor climbed into the pulpit and suggested remaining in the church until the drifting snow had eased. He pointed out the blankets, the cakes and the tea. At this prompt the helpers swarmed forth to provide for the audience. During this night this calm, peace and brightness remained. It was not wiped out by the rush of bringing the evening to a close. We played some more. This time nobody clapped, and not because the people hadn't liked it. It was if they had realized that this clapping basically ruins everything.

It is perhaps meant as sort of special payment - respect that is intended for the performer but which actually belongs to the music. The music itself, which doesn't want to hear itself distorted and disfigured by the rhythmic, ever louder clapping together of a multitude of hands in an ominous crescendo.

Its echo should be silence. An intimate listening together. Allowing the final sounds to resonate. We became one with the audience. When they no longer clapped us, holding us away as "the others", we grew towards each other, grew together. For every musician, for everyone who stands exposed on the stage, this is something quite special. So for all of us this became our silent, our holy night. Usually I keep away from such labels. I am a musician and not a pastor.

Perhaps, exceptionally, I am speaking on his behalf. He sat contentedly amongst the people, many of his parishioners were amongst them, and – during this night – he was able to simply be one of them. He suddenly looked decades younger – and decades, ages happier. I think that the responsibilities of this office are often a way heavier burden than people would ever imagine. Clearly I was not the only person to think so. We musicians looked at each other, understood each other without a word being spoken, and played the very last piece of this night for him. Of course we did not tell him this. Christmas Eve has always had something mysterious about it. And that is how we on this occasion wanted to leave it, according to tradition. Slowly the sounds died away, while the glow remained on the faces. It was one of my most solemn festivals, one of my most moving experiences as a musician. Agatha, my old teacher, who passed away years ago – in this night I saw as well - in my mind's eye. Our teachers are always with us; it is kind of a law.

Often not in a good way for they also thought us criticism and doubting ourselves.

With Agatha though it has always been different and has stayed it until now.

Whoever knew her would understand what I am talking about. Her radiance... no-one would be surprised to know, just could not be missed. Especially not in this very moment.

I wished here to be here and in a way I could clearly feel she was.

Count Zeppelin

It was in the old "Count Zeppelin-Hotel", or rather on the lower old green side-windows that adorned the dining room, at least in part. Here were numerous small figures to be seen, miniatures, people poured into the green, antique glass, who were busily engaged in some meaningful activity and who, as I thought, looked quite wonderful as they did so. Like little remnants from the past, figurines from a bygone era that must have been in so many ways so much more beautiful than ours.

My companion with whom I observed almost in an obsessed way the figurines from the outside, as we returned from our evening walk, did not agree at all. His gaze immediately, as seen before many times, caught a well known, certain characteristic in them, a common denominator:

"None of them laughs! "He stated, and as soon as he said that I noticed it too.

All the silly little joy collapsed in me. Yes. Their faces were tormented, pale and rigid. The eyes grim and wide. Life had obviously been difficult even then. We finally had a black tea in the lobby. The waiter, young, extremely handsome but strikingly pale and large-eyed with dark hair, looked just like one of the little figures out of the green window. The resemblance was so striking that my heart pounded right into my head. I secretly peeped over my companion's right shoulder to find out if one of the figures was missing or if there were an empty space in the glass - but the other half of his body was also hiding this very part of the window, and - you may forgive me for this - I did not like to ask him to stand up so that I could check and reassure myself. The waiter's eyes were also following me, so I had to be careful. Nobody should be suspicious. My companion was a rational person. What he might have just seen as a game, a nice little pastime (the conversation at the green window) - would, in view of such insistence, and almost pathological interest in this window might turn into dull and sheer incomprehension perhaps even to be followed by aggrieved rejection. I didn't want to risk that. The loneliness had been weighing heavily on me for some time, and so I was not in a free state to do or not to do just as I wished. The young waiter with the frozen face served us with a touch more frostiness than could be considered professional, almost with a hostility which I attributed to the fact the fact that I had presumably found out something about his monstrous secret. As expected, I slept badly that night, which my companion blamed on the nocturnal consumption of black tea.

We were on the second floor at an adequate distance to the green window on the ground floor. I let him sleep, enjoyed the warmth of his body, did not want to leave this warmth and could not have done otherwise in any case.

As soon as I could no longer bear the torturing uncertainty I slipped past the night porter, having hastily thrown on a few clothes, ran out to the sidewalk and looked at all the small figures that were adequately lit thanks to the milky glow of a lantern, coming gently from the opposite side of the street. Now I could get an exact picture. I saw the young waiter who was carrying out a different activity when captured in the glass. He was turning a spindle. The look, however, was the same. He stared rigidly right through me. Without thinking I gently placed the tip of my little finger on the glass, as if to stroke his cheek. Still, however, he silently looked through me. Didn't he notice me? The cold finally forced me back to the hotel, into the warm arms of my sleeping companion. The next morning the coffee was served to us by a young Russian woman. I looked around rather excitedly for the waiter, but he was nowhere to be seen. In front of the window inside the hotel, a Christmas tree was being put up so that I could not tell whether he was in the window or not. However, our place was placed diagonally to the tree, which gave me the chance to finally look at the window from the inside. I clearly saw it, the empty space in the window in which there now seemed to be a kind of bubble. My hands were trembling visibly. Meanwhile, my companion brought me rolls and all kinds of jam from the buffet. Only when he returned to me at the table again did I calm down down a little. I lost myself in his eyes until a familiar voice asked whether we might prefer tea instead of coffee. It was last night's waiter, the man from the glass. I took some, mainly to get rid of him, suddenly feeling somehow rather uncomfortable in his presence so that nodding was the easiest way. Finally he slowly disappeared behind one of the bars.

"What did you do to him?" my companion wanted to know." Why, what do you mean?" I felt somewhat surprised by his question. "Well, I don't know, I suddenly had the feeling that you had done something to him...", "But why?" He placed his hands on mine. "Just because he smiled today." "Oh." Now I smiled too. I said nothing more about it. After all, my companion is a rational person.

Kazimir and the ring

The first courageous act of my life, apart from that one to enter it at all, was to come to the aid of a raven who was in the unfortunate position of being pelted with stones by some of the neighbors' children. It didn't fly away, which surprised me. I have often wished for wings so that I could quickly escape in similarly depressing situations. He, on the other hand, did not seem to think about it at all. The poor raven sat all frozen with shock, rather uncharacteristically of a bird, and in doing so he did something that, given the situation, made me feel the sudden determination that made it possible for me to intervene. Nothing should happen to this raven.

Anyone who knows me would swear it couldn't have been me. They would have sworn that it must have been someone else who, armed with a large branch, threw himself screaming at the pack of neighboring children. But it was me, no one else. I, with holy anger, and thus actually able to drive away the mob. Nobody would have thought I could do that, least of all I would have believed myself.

But it was necessary for him. He still hadn't moved away, the raven, but now he was looking at me with undisguised curiosity, moving his little body a little to the side.

I approached him slowly and spoke quietly to him. After so many years I am not able to reproduce the exact wording, but it will essentially have been words of reassurance with the hint that the danger from the neighbors' children being finally over.

When repeating the good news seemed to me to be a bit lengthy itself over time, I decided to give the raven a name. From now on he was to be called Kazimir and, although looking back on things one cannot always be too sure, it seems to me that exactly this very moment was the beginning of our shy friendship. Whether it was because of him or the two of us, I can't say for sure. I suspect that we, obviously related in nature, were both a bit shy. Still, Kazimir followed me from that day.

He was waiting for me on the tree in front of the schoolyard. During the rather extended mornings, which sometimes (as generally known) seem endless, he helped me over many a long hour with Mr. Schaal. The school was new to me, the long sitting tormented me. Sometimes Kazimir accompanied me home and sometimes covered longer distances.

The raven appeared a few times suddenly in the Rosental and in the Auenwald; twice I saw him on a roof near the main train station and at least eight times he sat for several hours on the Bach monument while a concert was being given in the St. Thomas Church. He recognized me from the crowd of people, just as I found him again and again from the crowd of ravens. Kazimir sat most of the time, it is no longer possible for me to estimate how often this happened, on the tree directly in front of the balcony of our house. I often sat there to watch him. Here, in the sun, I didn't mind sitting. Above me the sky, it spread so wide and blue that the thought of the school that would start again soon seemed almost unreal to me. Nor did I understand in those moments that there was war.

We lived at war, and people were reminded so often that I was glad and relieved at every moment in which I could forget the war and watch Kazimir a little while flying or sitting near me. Only once, in the late summer before my seventh birthday, two days before starting school in the second grade, he suddenly came flying onto the parapet, puffed himself up briefly and then let something fall from his beak into my lap. It was a ring.

Not an expensive ring, it was made of brass and adorned with a small, light blue stone. Never again did Kazimir ever come as close to me again. After the event with the ring, I dreamed that Kazimir would sit on my shoulder and that I would be able to proudly walk through the city center with him. But this always remained a dream. Some things don't happen the way we think they should. I didn't go back to school long that fall. Many times I had feared the narrowness of the schoolhouse, the length of the mornings, instead it should hit me much harder now. I ended up in the children's hospital, more precisely in one of the scarlet barracks. Kazimir's ring was taken from me and I was told not to wear it for reasons of hygiene or at least some as disturbing reason.

But I thought, especially at this time, of the light blue color of the stone, which had the blue of a clear summer sky in it. These thoughts helped me more than I will be able to put into words. When I was in the scarlet barrack, the world seemed to have conspired against me. Apart from scarlet fever and the temporary loss of my ring. It started with the nurse, who apparently hated children. She wore a blonde bun and dragged her right leg a little. Even today I ask myself why such a person chooses the profession in which one has to do with children, with helpless and suffering children. Then, although I was already seven years old, I had to lie in a cot, just like the other children from the scarlet barracks. It was kind of more practical, but to me it was a grave shame. In addition to scarlet fever, I suffered from severe kidney infections, heart infections, and otitis media.

A short time ago I was completely healthy, but not only does hatred spread quickly during war. Hunger, hardship and severe disease some-times literally come overnight in a war. If we are already at night, I cannot avoid reporting from our nocturnal travels.

Unpleasant and deeply frightening journeys that were more like recurring nightmares. At night all children were taken to the air raid shelter. I was very scared of dying, but I didn't cry. Rather, I tried to be brave; I thought of Kazimir, of the blue of the ring, of my parents.

After all, I could see my parents behind a pane of glass during the day. Occasionally my mother tapped the window with her index finger as if to attract the attention of a trapped bird. And that was me. Kazimir's captive brother, deprived of his freedom and his ring. But one day, perhaps to let in air, a doctor had opened the window behind the dreary wall my parents stood in front of when they were allowed to see me. Now I looked outside behind them, saw a tree, a piece of heaven. It was draped with clouds, and yet a little bit of blue flashed from between the clouds. Not more than a streak, but enough to comfort me. And then I discovered something else, or rather - someone. I don't know if I can make it clear what it meant to me when I realized who it was, which guest had followed me all the way to the scarlet barracks. Kazimir.

Later, when I told the dubious nurse of all people about it, she claimed that there was no window in the corridor and that Kazimir was a product of my fever. I didn't believe her.

Involuntarily I touched the finger on which I had worn his ring, and I looked forward to the day when I would wear it again, when I would have been released from the scarlet barracks, when I would be back with my parents who would be at peace again and where Kazimir would be near me.

On a tree, a pole, in front of my balcony, in the rose valley, in the alluvial forest or on the Bach monument near the St. Thomas Church. He accompanied me for more than 12 years, witnessed more courageous as well as less courageous deeds of mine, Kazimir witnessed my life. Without him, I deeply am knowing this, would have missed something essential. I couldn't bury him because, although I felt he was dead, I never found him.

On the other hand, a raven like Kazimir may not need to be buried at all.

Because when I think of him I don't see a grave. I see the blue of a clear summer sky, see it get lighter and further.

He's in a good place now.
Nobody will throw stones at him where he is now. Nothing will hinder his flight, nor tarnish his happiness.

I always carry his ring with me.

The Garden

Even when I was a child people said of me that I was always laughing, and indeed everything in my life felt like laughter. Like laughter, warmth and sunlight. Then, I still remember it precisely because it was just before my 10th birthday, a sadness came over me that was so deep that I thought that if it ever went away again, it would also have taken my laughter away with it. I was terribly wrong for that quite astonishing reason I would like to make that clear from the start.

In the following years it kept coming back, as regular as any season.
Certainly the sadness kept returning too, but it became easier to bear through the knowledge that it would simply change places with my laughter which would then come back to me as secretly promised. This was how things stayed

until my mother died. From my mother's death onwards this laughter had gone away and it returned neither in the second nor in the following third year.

After the long winter that had followed the third year I got into a plane and flew, without any long previous deliberation to Sicily.

The tourist season had not properly begun, which suited me because I did not feel ready for all the bustling life that would be predominating at that time. It was nature alone that was already on the rise. Along the cliffs which led down to the sea I felt transported to a paradise garden:

African cedars, cacti, desert palms, lemon and orange trees, huge flowers and blossoms as close to the sky... At this sight my heart would beat faster and more strongly inside me. The sight was so beautiful that it was almost hurtful. The hotel was set on a rise so that I could look out to the Greek theatre and far out to sea. I often spent time in this part of the hotel with the best view as far as the snow-covered Etna. It was a quite special hotel. Everyone showed a great informal friendliness.

More than that. A young, obviously shy waiter with friendly, warm eyes - I liked him at once - every single day placed on my plate a flower that he had picked from the bushes growing outside the dining room. He only did that for me. As well as that, he brought me every day an extra bread-roll and an orange-blossom tea as if he were worried that I would not get enough to eat or to drink. Always, whenever he was nearby I felt safe. His kind actions were in no way obtrusive, in contrast to many of the actions of Sicilian men. I do not know the exact reason for it, but particularly the men from southern Italy feel especially attracted to me. Their gazes followed me in the dining room, in the street and even in church.

There was a little park there where I used to take refuge whenever this all became too much for me. And that is where I met him: a sun-tanned man with bright eyes, who inexplicably bore a Greek name even though, as he assured me, he was a Sicilian, fully certified and ennobled by the many generations that had lived here before him. He was old, and as I sat down next to him he sighed and said with a regret directed at myself how beautiful I was and he sighted with a self-accusatory "Why am I so old ? "Finally he gave up with a resigned shrug of his shoulders. "You don't laugh very much do you? " I nodded a bit in order to confirm this. "But laughter is the prerogative of the young, is it not?" "I have no experience of that", I reposted brusquely, since the point of this seemed to be eluding me. "I can give you back the laughter in your life, "he promised", because if you don't laugh then you don't live. So - in all humility – I can give you your life back." Involuntarily I thought back over all the moments when I had laughed. In my memory they arrayed themselves like pearls on the most beautiful necklace that had ever been seen.

But in the meantime they had disappeared from view, an unknown thief had taken them from me, as it now seemed in a rather undeniably way.

Out of the blue this old man, rather sly-looking and to judge from the state of his skin about 300 years old was now seriously going to snatch them back from this thief for me ? What would he want in return? The fact that nothing in life is free I knew already. "What have you to lose then? "The old man now wanted to know disarmingly. Tired from the unaccustomed warmth and from the heavy scents of the tropical garden, I gave in.

And this day, followed by the night, he returned not just the necklace to me. It was a neverending treasure-trove of warm sparkling laughter, of the scent of southern fruits and of a light, warm wind that wafted in from the sea and stroked my skin.

A nightingale I could hear as well far, far way, soft in the distance. I have promised to give away nothing about this night, but it contained something as a treasure was preserved within it. The essence of my life - compressed into these few hours of a single night. Of one day and one night. When in the morning I returned to my hotel I noticed that something had changed. Men no longer gazed after me, they did not wave from cars or buses, and they did not call out to me across the street, no longer whistled after I had passed by. I was surprised that these forms of attention were mysteriously missing, but as well as this I realised that, strangely, I suddenly missed them, something that saddened me a little.

The steep path leading up to the hotel also seemed considerably more arduous than the previous time. I managed to sneak slowly but unnoticed into my room since the reception desk was generally not manned at breakfast-time. Even the stairs seemed unaccustomedly tiring. Opening the door, I glanced at the hand which was holding the key. It was a hand, but not mine. As quickly as I could, I hurried into the bathroom because a terrible suspicion had arisen in me which was crushing all the life within. The view in the mirror confirmed this hunch and I cannot say how I managed to get into my bed without screaming in horror. In only one night I had become an old woman. The mysterious man had returned my life to me but at the same time made me pay for it with its very self.

A monstrous rage surged up inside me in a gigantic wave which then collapsed into itself. In the bed, covered by the white sheet. I felt my strength fading and my resentment towards the old man was now no more than a soft echo.

He had cheated me of nothing. Much more had had given me the portion of laughter that my life had been holding in readiness for me. But he had jumped over the periods of drought in between, the dark chapters. Yes he might have cheated me of these but personally

I found that there were worse crimes than this. There could be, I admit, mixed opinions about that. He had leafed through the pages of my book of life at such a furious pace; and every page that had contained some laughter. He had read aloud to me, laughed for me, figuratively danced for me.

I looked again at my hands. The fragile hands of an old woman, crossed by these inevitable lines like a marble dish that had been broken and then stuck back together as a makeshift repair. None of the beautiful young men who even yesterday had thought of me with their languishing damp eyes and sighing promises would no longer wish to touch this hand, these hands, of their own free will. That must be a dream - might it be? Could something like this really happen? I felt so dizzy, so sad and so weak in my heart. There was a cautious knock at the door. I called out something like "Come in! "And the young waiter with the friendly dark eyes was standing there with a bread-roll, the tea and a flower, which contrasted magically with the dark colour of the tray. He smiled as radiantly as ever, sat down on the edge of the bed, without hesitating took it, this tiny, old hand as if it were something infinitely valuable and kissed it. "I think I shall die today "I said to him. "As well, I am not sure that I can still eat this bread-roll here... non ho fame. "

The liveliness of the melodious Italian language again contradicted the words just used.

My voice died away, was little more than a tentative whisper.

The he placed the flower in my hand, nodded and kissed my brow.

"It is all a dream, Cara "he said gently. "Everything is a dream."

I closed my eyes but still sensed that he was sitting next to me and was watching over my sleep. Would I wake up again? I did not know. But as the awareness of the first dream of this already warm morning settled on me I heard it again.

The immortal laughter from the garden in which I had spent the night.

On the window

The little blue tit lay dead on its back, its little claws reaching towards the sky. I had still heard the cracking, muffled sound on the window pane and prayed that it was not what it sounded like. But such prayers did not help against glass that was too clean.

On one of the last days of November, which had not yet quite reached the consolation of December, this rapid dying had occurred outside my window. I carefully buried it in the not yet frozen ground. It was a mild November. Early on, the crow, the magpie and the squirrel had fought over the nuts I had thrown into the front garden, and before long all the titmouse dumplings that should have lasted me until late January had been eaten. In vain. It was also in vain that I had fed her, the little blue tit - that was such a pity. I immediately decided to buy Christmas decorations to put on the windows so that the birds would be warned. If it had been my own home, I would have thought of something earlier, but I was only a guest here and was not allowed to change anything accordingly. Such is the fate of eternal guests. I quickly found what I was looking for in the shop and carried two rolls of window pictures into the house with me.

The easily removable hosts of silver plastic snowflakes, paired with several green trees, a reindeer, a candle in red and a Father Christmas, were not necessarily stylish, but they would save lives.

When I have to leave here again, maybe in spring, I'll just take them with me, my stickers, and who knows, maybe I'll take them all with me. All the birds from this garden. I'm imagining it now, while the squirrel, crow and magpie are still squabbling over the nuts. In fact, I don't have many left. Will we all make it through the winter? I can't say.

At the window I discover another small, isolated and trembling tiny feather.

The watchmaker's daughter

"Please draw a clock here!" The psychologist pushed a sheet of paper to Josefa; she was already holding the pencil, and just as she had always been told never to let it out of her hand, never to relinquish control, she held it tightly while she tried very hard to put a somewhat neat clock face down on paper.

Josefa knew that this was a test for dementia, so she tried particularly hard, as if she could draw away the increasing forgetfulness that had spread in her life, as if everything would be all right again if the psychologist would only praise her, and, perhaps even himself relieved, write or simply tick off something like "not demented" on his diagnosis pad. But - despite all her efforts - she did not succeed. Even the even division of the time units, indicated by the lines round the circumference to her regret did not succeed, not to mention the numbers. She would have preferred to cry, but instead continued to cling to her pencil Just don't lose control. The psychologist made a note and tried to come to her aid.

"What time is it on that clock?" He pointed to a painted clock face with an hour and minute hand with his bushy eyebrows raised questioningly. Josefa now found it even harder to concentrate.
What could he have written down? Now that it was there on a piece of paper, was it official and therefore a reality?

"A quarter to three". Josefa had decided to say just anything. Something that sounded like a normal description of the time. Maybe she was lucky, and chance would have it that the time shown on the paper and the time she had guessed coincided. The psychologist shook his head while placing a tick on his paper. Josefa felt anger rising inside her. If anyone knew anything about clocks, it was probably her! But the anger collapsed again before it could really unfold and gave way to something else.

Josefa, shrunken back to a young, frightened woman, felt trapped in her thoughts again in a deformed, jagged pocket watch, more reminiscent of a dragon.

She no longer knew what time it was? She of all people, didn't remember? What a bitter irony. Josefa was the only daughter of a well-known watchmaker who had since died. For a long time now, only the clocks bore witness to his former presence, reminding us through their symbolism of the fundamental transience of things, without, however, expressing anything fundamentally new. But despite his death, they continued to tick after him for many decades, in every musical key and each in its own way: His clocks and watches.

The dials, circular like the snake biting its own tail, revealed more than one would have known even without them. The timepieces ticked and whirred in their house, struck and cracked, sounded and rattled. It had been going on for almost a hundred years now. Clocks from the 15th century, ornate wall clocks, train and pendulum clocks, world clocks, Persian desert clocks, also called sand clocks, timers and original skeleton clocks, countless regulators, English mantel clocks, traditional dark and also more modern, brightly painted black-and-walnut clocks in every conceivable
size with variations as far as Christmas clocks.

There were watches with roman and arabic numerals, unbelievably expensive Swiss watches with unshakable movements, very special watches with Breguet hands, with Cabochan and manual winding, expensive wristwatches with sapphire crystal, selected jewellery watches with numerous filigree baguette movements very specially made for women, numerous savo-nettes, ornate and engraved silver and gold pocket watches for the self-respecting gentle-men. There were pilot's watches, chronographs, even watches with an integrated "perpetual calendar". Admittedly: In the course of time, most of them had fallen silent. Josefa had forgotten to wind them up, but that didn't change the fact that she had spent her whole life with clocks. She still remembered the constant ticking, the reassuring companions of her childhood. Now, on the other hand, there was truly little that was reassuring. Losing one's memory was not exactly pleasant. It was threatening, frightening, like a clock that had stopped, that you no longer knew how to wind, and that you couldn't get to start again, even with the best of coaxing. Yes, it wasn't just that Josefa had forgotten to wind her clocks lately. It wasn't just that, she simply didn't know how to do it anymore. Tears welled up in her eyes and the sudden look she gave the young psychologist had something devastating about it. It was difficult for her to deal with the other questions of the test and with disdain she noticed the cheap-looking digital watch on the psychologist's wrist.

So this philistine would sit in judgement on her.

As he spoke, something in her refused to listen. He spoke and spoke, steady as one of the ticking clocks of her childhood. Meanwhile, still oblivious to the words, she felt herself growing quiet. She no longer spoke, sank into herself and finally fell completely silent - like one of the many beautiful and venerable clocks which she had not wound up lately. The young psychologist hesistated but then did not dare to disturb her nor to intervene with her endearing silence.

Alyosha and Katya

Alyosha and Katya were a couple as rarely seen before. Alyosha loved Katya as only very few could. Not that Katya didn't deserve that love. I don't mean that. Everyone deserves love, although that may not be the right word. But a very few people are unfortunately able to love their own kind truly and from the heart. It was different with Alyosha and Katya. He did everything to make sure that no branch got in front of her head, no stone got in front of her shoe. He looked after her where he could, tucked her in on the cold nights and thanked life every single day for giving him Katya. It was the same the other way round.

Nothing would have made Katya think poorly of her Alyosha, just the thought of him made her want to be alive. He gave her flowers, which she put by the window. With no one else did they stay in bloom as well as with her. Alyosha and Katya loved and needed each other, and even after years they could not take their eyes off each other. It looked as if their happiness was one of those that would last. Unfortunately, it was not to be. Something quite inexplicable happened on one of the coldest nights that 1893 had in store for St. Petersburg. All of a sudden the fire in was no longer burning, so Alyosha went to have a look. He spent half an hour or so outside, balancing on the roof, ducking under the howling wind and finally freeing the chimney from a branch that had broken through all the snow, until everything was back in order.

He had never been so cold. Katya heated the stove until late at night and rubbed Alyosha's cold hands warmly so that he would quickly forget the cold. She took great pains for she felt something had happened, desperately hoping for it to pass.

But the very next morning Alyosha was still different. The old order was out of balance. All love had left him all at once. He could no longer look at Katya with the eyes of love. Rather, she suddenly appeared to him to be an evil, vile woman. He also no longer liked the way she looked. Wasn't she clearly too small, her hair too dark?

Katya was shocked as she had never been before when she read the sudden coldness in his gaze, the stiffness of his features, in which now the only expression left was a slightly contemptuous tug around his mouth. Even his skin seemed cool and pale. Katya prepared hot drinks and meals for him, brought him blankets and hot compresses. But Alyosha pushed everything away, just as he pushed Katya away. With each sad winter day that passed, he grew colder and colder, and it was only cold that he could bear. When Katya wanted to embrace him as she used to, the warmth of her palm hurt him so much that he pushed her away violently until she fell to the ground.

Katya thought of a fairy tale she had read a long time ago about a shard of ice that had to be pulled out of the victim's back in such a case. But there was no shard. Moreover, Alyosha would not have allowed Katya to approach him so closely. Even if she stood a metre in front of him, he could not bear the warmth that emanated from her. No matter how hard Katya tried, she could not think of a solution. Then, on a sad, remarkably harsh, icy December night, Alyosha disappeared forever. It is said that Father Frost needed a helper. Katya, who had stayed behind alone, often called for him. But nothing but ice flowers appeared at the window through which he had climbed on the longest night of the year. So wonderfully were they drawn. Like images of the flowers Alyosha had given her in earlier times. Katya laid her warm hands gently on them.

Hector

Johann remembered in detail the first Christmas Eve after the death of his wife.

He had trudged through the snow alone, meanwhile also without his little dog, who, he suspected out of sheer grief, had followed his Agnes only two months later.

So for nine months he was all alone, without Agnes and Hector, and he had never felt so lonely in his life. It was snowing heavily and the landscape was reminiscent of a sugary tale from a fairy story. The pure joy of Christmas seemed to seep through to him from the lighted and festively decorated windows. What a contrast to what he had now. Gone was all joy.

It had died first with Agnes and then, once more and finally, with Hector. Music and laughter filled the streets nevertheless.

Christmas joys. A joy he could no longer take part in. The snowflakes danced over his face and mixed there with tears that he thought were his business alone. He thought hard about Agnes and about Hector. So firmly and so exclusively that there was no room for mourning.

Eventually he decided to end the walk and return to his house. Even from afar he didn't find it tempting. It stood before him cold and empty, the windows nothing but eyes without sight. He lowered his head, which he always did when he wanted to gain courage. In such situations, he often bowed his head and then raised it in a flash to give himself courage. For Agnes and for Hector he would walk straight into this house. He thought about them all the time. It was snowing less heavily now. As he stood, head bowed, waiting for his inner strength to lift him up, he saw something in the snow. He trembled because he didn't believe what he saw, And yet it was there. There were footprints in the snow. Right next to his.

But he was sure that he had no companion during the entire time of his nocturnal walk.

But nevertheless. Quite clearly and parallel to his footprints he saw a smaller pair close to his. And then, to the right of these, there were paw prints in the snow. Agnes had always walked to his right, Hector to her right.

"Come into the house, at least today," he asked into the stillness of the night. Soon a light was seen, which Johann had lit in the house. The curtains were not closed and he was seen moving about the house. From the sofa To the table, to the kitchen, to the table again. Everything indicated that he was alone. But there were three sets of footprints all the way to his door. The snow was about to bury them all. But if you looked closely then you could still clearly see the imprint of a small dog's paw.

**Claudia J. Schulze**: Studied literature, psychology, cognitive sciences and philosophy in Freiburg, Zurich, Karlsruhe and Constance. Degree in educational psychology with literature didactics, doctorate in Freiburg.

Member of the editorial board of the literary magazine WANDLER. Member of the Constance authors group "Literary Café" and the Steinbach Ensemble (Baden-Baden)

Publication of several short stories as well as poetry and excerpts from longer stories in various literary magazines in Germany, Austria and Switzerland (Wandler, CET, Am Zeitstrand, decision, anthologies such as the library of German-language poems. Audiobooks ("In the Shoes of the World", "Night Flights") Print & Online Publications, Print-On-Demand. Publication of several reviews (print and online), library of German-language poems, slam poetry, numerous groups of authors and literary blogs, focus: Russian classics.

Andrew Timothy Holden, London & Berlin Musician: (Tim Holden), Feel free to check:

 ath

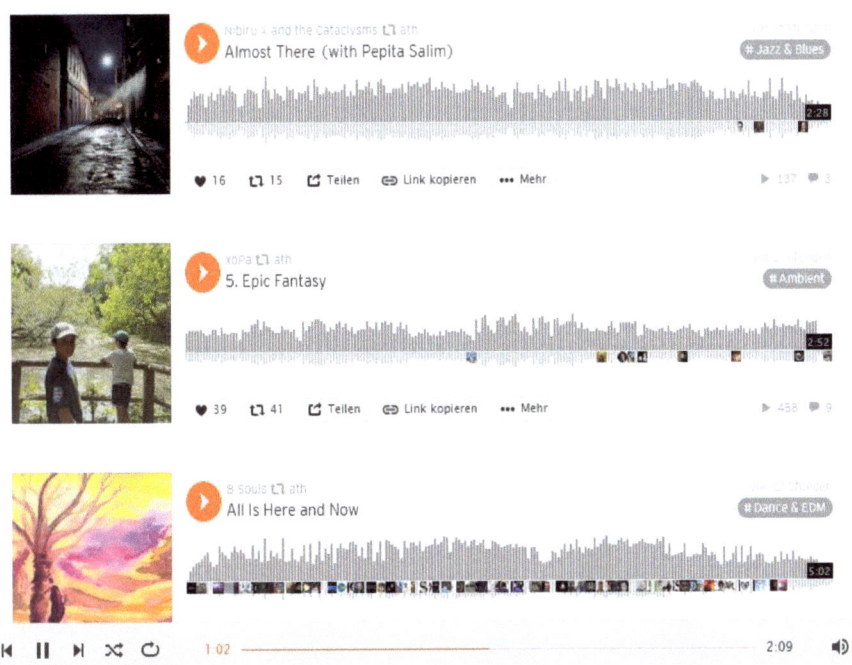

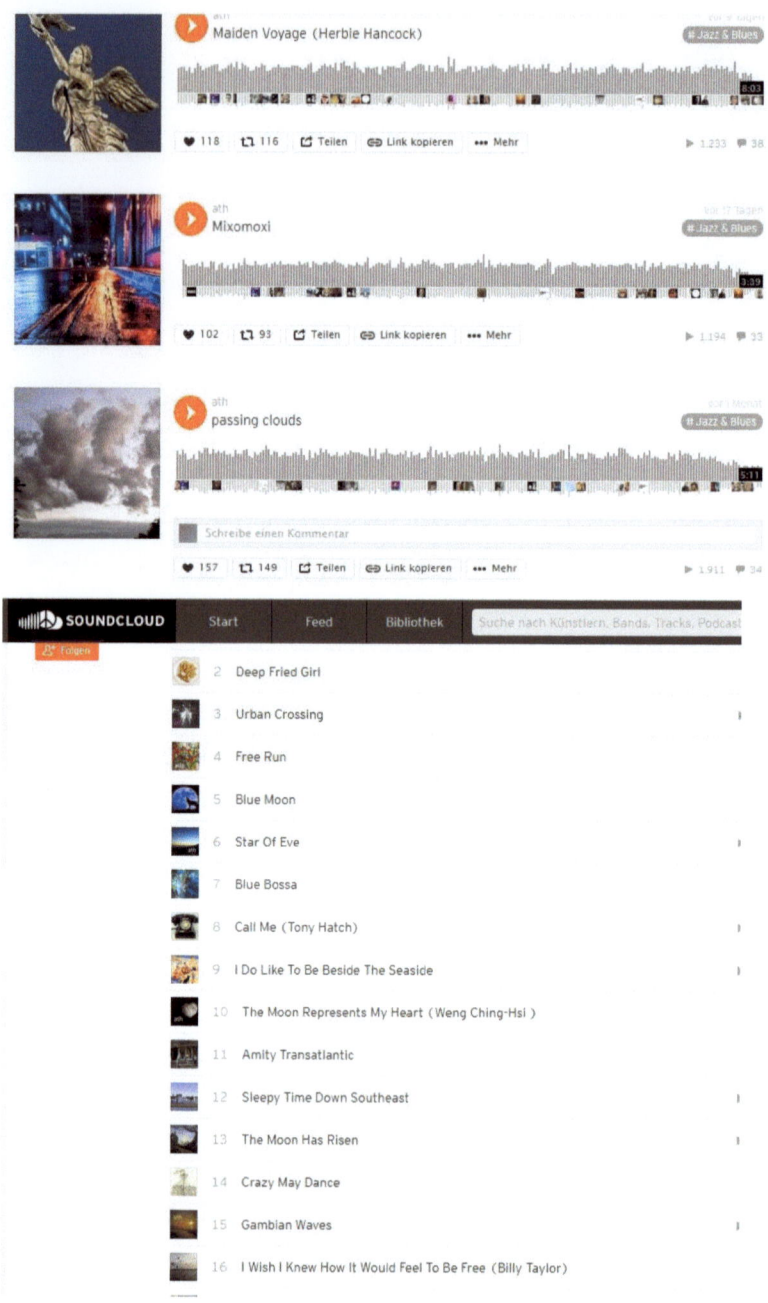

> I no doubt deserved my enemies, but I don't believe I deserved my friends.
>
> Walt Whitman

Thank you, dear Tim, Michael and Vita!

Pictures by Vita Tucaite and Mike Douglas Crawley

Michael Douglas Crawley, Lexington, Indiana, U.S.A.&

Vita Tucaite, Vilnius, Lithuania